Ladybug Baby Bug

by

Janice and Mark Perkins

AuthorHouse™
1663 Liberty Drive, Suite 200
Bloomington, IN 47403
www.authorhouse.com
Phone: 1-800-839-8640

AuthorHouse™ UK Ltd.
500 Avebury Boulevard
Central Milton Keynes, MK9 2BE
www.authorhouse.co.uk
Phone: 08001974150

First published by AuthorHouse 3/15/2007

ISBN: 978-1-4259-9546-1 (sc)

Printed in the United States of America
Bloomington, Indiana

This book is printed on acid-free paper.

Bloomington, IN   Milton Keynes, UK

authorHOUSE®

Dedication

Dedicated to our grandsons,
Austin and Jordan

My name is LADYBUG BABY BUG. When I wake up, I call for my MOMMA BUG. She gives me a kiss and asks me if I want some breakfast.

Sometimes, MOMMA BUG makes oatmeal. Sometimes she makes pancakes, but French toast is LADYBUG BABY Bug's favorite.

When I get thirsty, I call for my DA-DA BUG. He hugs me and brings LADYBUG BABY BUG a bottle.

When I want to play, I call my SISSY BUG. She counts for LADYBUG BABY BUG and says the A, B, Cs. Then we play with my toys.

Then I call my NA-NA BUG and she rocks LADYBUG BABY BUG. She sings, "I love my LADYBUG BABY BUG," until I fall asleep.

When I wake up from my nap, I call my PA-PA BUG and he hugs me and takes me for a walk.

On the walk, I see my friends, BUTTERFLY BABY FLY and BUMBLE BEE BABY BEE.

When I get home, I call for my
BROTHER BUG and he colors with
LADYBUG BABY BUG. I love to color
flowers.

Then MOMMA BUG puts me to bed and I think about MOMMA BUG, DA-DA BUG, SISSY BUG,

NA-NA BUG, PA-PA BUG, and BROTHER BUG. LADYBUG BABY BUG is so happy because LADYBUG BABY BUG loves her family.